Maui-Maui

Written by Stephen Cosgrove
Illustrated by Robin James

A Serendipity™ *Book*

PSS!
PRICE STERN SLOAN

The Serendipity™ series was created by Stephen Cosgrove and Robin James.

Copyright © 1995, 1979 by Price Stern Sloan. All rights reserved.
Published by Price Stern Sloan, a division of
Penguin Putnam Books for Young Readers, New York.

Printed in Hong Kong. Published simultaneously in Canada. No part of this publication may be
reproduced, stored in any retrieval system, or transmitted, in any form or by any means, electronic,
mechanical, photocopying, recording, or otherwise, without the prior written permission of the
publisher.

ISBN 0-8431-3829-7
2002 Printing

PSS! is a registered trademark of Penguin Putnam Inc.
Serendipity™ and the pink dragon are trademarks of Penguin Putnam Inc.

Library of Congress Cataloging-in-Publication Data

Cosgrove, Stephen.
Maui-Maui / written by Stephen Cosgrove; illustrated by Robin James.
p. cm.
"A Serendipity Book"
Summary: A whale teaches the Amomonies to respect the balance of nature and take only
what they need from the sea.
ISBN 0-8431-3829-7
[1. Fishery conservation—Fiction. 2. Marine resources conservation—Fiction. 3. Whales—
Fiction.] 1. James, Robin, ill. II. Title.
PZ7.C8187Mau 1995
[Fic]—dc20   94-21449
                                                                              CIP
                                                                              AC

Dedicated to the Lahaina Restoration Society and their exceptional marine program: WHALE WATCHERS. Jim Luckey and his dedicated staff taught me the true value of Maui-Maui and all the other magnificent whales of the world.

—*Stephen*

To learn how you can help with conserving and saving the wonderful world of the whales, write to:
SAVE THE WHALES
P.O. Box 3650, Washington D.C. 20007

eagulls soared over the clear blue waters of the Pacific Ocean. Their wings dipped and tipped the waves as the wind gently floated them to unknown destinations.

Suddenly the stillness of the ocean was broken by the mighty leap of a whale as it breached high into the air and crashed back into the sea. Soon the water was awash as an entire pod of whales flipped and frolicked in the crystal morning sunshine.

They floated and rolled in the sea, spouting water high into the air, and basked in the sunshine shower of rainbows they had created. The warm air nearly lulled the whales to sleep as they drifted gently in the blue Pacific waters.

Far off on the horizon, a dozen or so strange little boats suddenly appeared. The quiet solitude of the whales was broken by the loud, squeaky voices of small, furry creatures called Amomonies, who manned the sails on the strange little boats.

The whales, with an unspoken signal, slid beneath the surface of the sea and quickly swam away.

The Amomonies, with much arm-waving, screaming, and yelling, threw their nets into the water and began the daily chore of fishing.

As soon as the nets were filled with fish, the Amomonies pulled them aboard, dumped the fish into the bottom of the boat, and tossed the nets back into the water. Their nets caught everything and anything: little fish, big fish, tuna, cod, and even an occasional octopus that had the misfortune to be swimming by. The Amomonies really didn't care. They just threw them into the bottom of the boat, tossed the nets back into the water, and fished some more.

They were always in such a hurry to catch a bunch of fish that one, or sometimes two, of the Amomonies would slip on a fish and fall into the water, getting caught in the net. It didn't matter to the other Amomonies; they would just haul in the nets and dump their soggy friend into the bottom of the boat with all the fish. Poor Amomony! He'd shake the water out of his fur, brush off the seaweed, climb back up onto the deck of the ship, and fish some more.

They fished like this for hours and hours. Waving their arms, screaming and yelling, the Amomonies threw the nets into the water and filled them with fish, hauled in the nets, and dumped the fish into the bottom of the boat. Then they started all over again.

When their boats couldn't hold another fish without sinking, they finally set their sails and headed back to Amomony Island.

When they arrived back at their island, the other Amomonies helped them drag their boats onto the beach and unload all the fish they had caught. There were so many fish, baskets and baskets of them, that nobody cared when a little stray kitten snatched one and hightailed it to the other side of the island.

When all the fish were cleaned, the queen of all the Amomonies, Mom Amomony, would cook the most delicious dishes you could ever imagine. She would cook fish stew, fried fish, fricasseed fish, roast fish, fish soup, and best of all, for dessert, fresh fish pudding with seasoned seaweed sauce. Mom Amomony, just like the other Amomonies who always caught more fish than they could use, always cooked more fish than they could eat. It doesn't matter, they thought. There are always more fish in the sea.

Once again, the very next morning, the Amomonies boarded their boats and set sail for new fishing grounds.

When they arrived, they began yelling, screaming, and waving their arms as they threw their nets into the sea. But before they had a chance to pull in the first net of fish, a large, magnificent whale breached high into the air, and crashed down on the Amomonies' nets.

Try as they might, the Amomonies could not haul in their nets with that monstrous whale holding on to the other end. They tugged and pulled to no avail. Finally, out of frustration, they cut the nets free and watched the fish sink to the bottom of the ocean.

The Amomonies sat around on their gently rocking boats trying to figure out what to do.

They thought and thought and then one of the creatures said brightly, "I know! We've all got our old fishing poles aboard. If we can't net the fish, we can catch them with hook, line, and sinker."

Hmmm! thought the other Amomonies. It may take a little longer but we can still fill our boats with fish.

So they hurriedly gathered all the poles together, tied the hooks onto the lines, and cast them into the water. Just as one of the little creatures was about to hook the first fish, that very same whale came slipping up and out of the water, and snatched the pole right out of his hands!

"This will never do!" they cried as they threw their poles down in disgust. "We must go back to the island and ask the queen what to do." With that they hurriedly set sail for home.

Well, as usual when the boats returned, the other Amomonies rushed out to help unload all the fish that had been caught. Much to their dismay there wasn't a single fish to unload.

"What's the meaning of this?!" shouted Mom Amomony.

The fishermen all knelt at her feet and cried, "We tried, oh great queen, but whenever we tried to catch any fish, a mighty whale would steal our nets and our fishing poles. We didn't know what we should do."

"Poppycock!" grumbled the queen. "First thing in the morning I will sail out and talk to this mighty whale of yours and I'll command him to leave you alone." With that she stomped back to her hut to prepare for the journey.

Bright and early the next morning, the queen of all the Amomonies set out to find the great whale. She sailed all morning and long into the day but nowhere could she find the whale.

"Those lazy fishermen probably made up the whole thing. There isn't any whale at all!" Then, just to prove her point, she decided to fish for a little while. With much yelling, screaming, and waving of her arms she threw her net over the side of the boat. Before the net even touched the water, the great whale leaped high into the air and landed on top of the net.

"Now see here!" she shouted haughtily. "Why are you doing that? Give me back my net; I am causing you no harm!"

"Oh, but you are," said the whale. "My name is Maui-Maui and I am the leader of a small pod of whales who live peacefully in these waters. We didn't mind when you moved to the island and began to fish in the sea. But now, because of your wastefulness, there aren't enough fish for my fellow whales and we are going hungry."

"Oh, pooh!" grumbled Mom Amomony.
"There have always been plenty of fish in the
sea. I'll tell you what Master Maui-Maui, I will
swim with you and you may show me." With
that she removed her seashell cape and her palm
leaf crown and leaped bravely into the water
with the great whale.

"As you wish," said Maui-Maui quietly. "But
I swim much faster than you. Hold on to my
dorsal fin and I will show you an empty sea."

The queen did as he asked and they sank
into the deep blue water. Down and down they
went, and all the while they saw not one fish of
any type, not even a single, solitary octopus.

Deeper and deeper they went and still not one fish was seen. Finally, after searching every nook and cranny at the bottom of the sea, they surfaced near the queen's boat and Maui-Maui carefully helped her onto the deck.

"I don't understand," she said as she combed the seaweed from her hair. "There used to be so many fish. Where have they all gone?"

Maui-Maui thought for a moment and then carefully replied, "You always caught more fish than you needed and you always cooked more fish than you needed. Now, because of your wastefulness there aren't any fish at all."

"What are we to do?" she cried. "Without the fish we will surely starve."

"Come," said the great whale, "let me tow you back to your island and I will teach you and your people how to share your life with the sea." He carefully slipped the net over his head and quickly pulled the small boat back to the island.

SO WHEN YOU ARE OUT FISHING

IN THE OCEANS, LAKES, OR SEAS,

REMEMBER MAUI-MAUI AND

THE LESSON OF THE AMOMONIES.

Serendipity™ Books

Created by
Stephen Cosgrove and Robin James

Enjoy all the delightful books in the Serendipity™ Series:

Available wherever books are sold.

PSS!
PRICE STERN SLOAN